The Bear's Bicycle

The Bear's Bicycle

by

EMILIE WARREN McLEOD

Illustrated by

DAVID McPHAIL

LITTLE, BROWN AND COMPANY
New York Boston

Other books by David McPhail
THE BEAR'S TOOTHACHE
LOST
SANTA'S BOOK OF NAMES

Little, Brown and Company

Hachette Book Group
237 Park Avenue, New York, NY 10017
Visit our website at www.lb-kids.com

Little, Brown and Company is a division of
Hachette Book Group, Inc.
The Little, Brown name and logo are trademarks of
Hachette Book Group, Inc.

First Paperback Edition: October 1986
First published in hardcover in April 1975 by
Little, Brown and Company

ISBN 978-0-316-56206-5

HC: 10 9 8 7 6
PB: 20

SC
MANUFACTURED IN CHINA

Library of Congress Cataloging-in-Publication Data

McLeod, Emilie Warren.
 The bear's bicycle.

 SUMMARY: A boy and his bear have an exciting
bicycle ride.
 [1. Bicycles and bicycling—Fiction] I. McPhail,
David M., ill. II. Title.
PZ7.M22496Bc3   [E]   74-28282
ISBN 978-0-316-56206-5

For Stuart M.
and to Sally L.

Every afternoon we go bike riding.

I check the tires   and the brakes
and make sure the handlebars turn.

Then I get on my bike and coast down the driveway.
At the end of the driveway I look to the right and to the left.

I make the hand signal for a right turn and I turn right.

If I have to cross the street I stop and get off my bike.
I look both ways.
If no cars are coming I walk my bike across the street.

I watch for car doors that are open.

I steer around cans and broken glass.

I stop for dogs to make sure they are friendly.

When I meet another bike I stay to the right.

And when I come up behind people I warn them
so they can get out of the way.

When I go down a hill I don't go too fast

and I use my brakes.

I always start home before it is dark

and put away my bike.

I wipe my feet before going in the house.

Then we have milk and crackers.